Dickinson

BEAR

APOCALYPSE

Ursine Abominations of the End Times and How to Defeat Them

ETHAN NICOLLE

"The morning was bright and propitious. Before their departure, mass had been said in the chapel, and the protection of St. Ignatius invoked against all contingent evils, but especially against bears, which, like the fiery dragons of old, seemed to cherish unconquerable hostility to the Holy Church."

- Bret Harte
The Legend Of Monte Del Diablo

www.Bearmageddon.com
www.BearmageddonNews.com
www.EthanNicolle.com

Ethan Nicolle - *Lead Writer / Artist*
Rachel Davey - *Research / Assistant Writer*
Austin Vashaw - *Editor*

ISBN-13: 978-1535080491
ISBN-10: 1535080493

Contents

Foreword by AXE COP

Bears are huge and they can run as fast as horses. Shooting them with a gun only makes them more angry. Blowing them up works sometimes, but you have to hide the TNT inside of a large salmon, and salmon is really slippery, besides, it makes your hands smell gross. And we must be aware that sometimes, when you explode a bear, it turns into a thousand smaller bears, which then rapidly grow into super bears. Super bears can never die and they can eat cities. They have two stomachs, one for bodies, the other for souls so that their prey will never reach the afterlife.

Bears are the only animal that take more than one chop of my axe. They take 100 chops, minimum. I can chop really fast, but that's still a lot of chopping. If you try to use a flamethrower on a bear, all of their fur will burn off and poisonous spikes will release from their bodies. They've been waiting there all along to poke people and kill them. A cannon may be useful. But bears are really good at catching cannonballs in their mouths. If they do this, they will turn the cannon ball into a bomb and shoot it back at you. Pirates learned this the hard way, hence they are now extinct. Only the greatest swordsman on earth could cut a bear with a sword. He did, and he was eaten immediately afterwards.

Bears cannot drown. When God flooded the earth, bears didn't die. They just hibernated because floods are boring to bears. If you push a bear into a volcano, you will clog it up, and lava will erupt out of the other side of the earth and kill thousands of people. If you freeze a bear, they will only eventually kill future civilizations that have invented time travel and come back and kill you. You cannot poison bears. Poison is their favorite food. When they eat it, people they stare at die instantly because it gives them poison staring.

The only way to get a bear to be on your team is to go to the God of all Bears and make an offering, but it has to be something extravagant, like honey from the god of all bees or a salmon-tailed mermaid. In this book you will learn about the many kinds of bears who will take over the world when Bearmageddon happens. I hope you enjoy this book, and remember that you will die from bears.

-Axe Cop, July, 2016

Bearilla
(Ursus Fentonus)

Bearillas are ground-dwelling ursine apes that have been seen in various parts of the world. They are the largest living primates, even larger than the silverback gorilla of central Africa. The DNA of bearillas is similar to that of a gorilla and bear, but vastly different from a human.

Though bearillas' natural habitats should be tropical or subtropical forests in Africa, they tend to prefer clearing out grocery stores and fried chicken restaurants and claiming them for their own.

Bearillas who live in the wild tend to prefer to dwell at high elevations, on top of volcanoes. They like to do cannonballs into the hot lava. This activates the volcano and the creatures surf on their rear paws as the flowing molten rock destroys everything in its path.

Bearillas punch incredibly hard, often turning a victim's skull into dust on the first strike. However, they can be a playful species as they have been known to floss their teeth with the intestines of their prey, or strum them like guitar strings.

How to defeat them: Your only option is to try to feed them bombs.

Octobear
(Ursus octopus vulgaris)

Octobears are among the most intelligent and behaviorally diverse of all bears. They can swim, travel on land, climb trees, walls, and hide where least expected, for example, in sewers or in the dark corners of ceilings. Anywhere tentacles can stick an octobear can be found.

The octobear has eight large tentacles that can crush bones into splinters with a few easy twists. The octobear's skeleton can become malleable, giving it the ability to fit through tight spaces. They have numerous tactics for attacking their prey, including the expulsion of acidic ink, the use of camouflage and deimatic behavior, shape changing, stretching, and a venomous harpoon that emerges from their tongue. They can jet quickly through water and can hide incredibly well for a creature their size. They can fit through any hole because they have gelatinous bones. They have been known to climb into people's face holes then tear them apart from the inside.

The octobear hunts around the clock, mostly in dark places. It prefers human meat but may settle for farm or zoo animals if driven by hunger. Sea dwelling octobears live mostly on a steady diet of shark. The octobear can change color to blend in with its surroundings, and its coiled tentacles make it able to pounce with the speed of a bear trap.

How to defeat them: The octobear's tentacles are easy to slice off with a sharp blade and will shrivel up in the heat. You can also feed it bombs.

Left: *An octobear extracted from a sewer in Northern California. The creature had the remains of seven humans, four cats, thirty seven chickens, and a donkey in its stomach. The creature died choking on a chicken bone.*

Below:

A rare image of Axe Cop battling an octobear at the fighting zoo. Axe Cop won, but after the battle he said, "I saved some of the octobear's blood. I think I may sprinkle some on Flute Cop because an octobear would make a really good cop."

Above: *A rare depiction of Axe Cop riding a tame bear elk while killing ninjas. This has never been accomplished by anyone else and is not recommended.*

Bear Elk

(Ursus cervus canadensis)

The bear elk possesses an even number of toes on each foot, similar to those of camels, goats and cattle, except it has really huge sharp claws. Unlike normal elk, the bear elk is carnivorous. It is a ruminant species, with a four-chambered stomach. One for boiling, one for squishing, one for grinding, and one for turning into vapor. All of the bear elk's waste is emitted as a gas, causing the animal to release a foul odor almost constantly. The bear elk consumes between four and seven forest animals or people a day.

Bear elk are more than twice as heavy as non-bear elk. Like elk, bear elk may gather in herds. Females average 896 to 1031 lb, stand 6.3 ft at the shoulder, and are 8.9 ft from nose to tail. Males are some 40% larger than females at maturity, weighing an average of 1405 to 1430 lb, standing 6.9 ft at the shoulder and averaging 11 ft in length. The point is, they're really big.

Only the males have antlers, which start growing in the spring and are shed each winter. While actively growing, the antlers are covered with and protected by a soft layer of highly vascularised skin known as velvet. Once fully grown the antlers can be used to stab multiple victims at the same time, and could easily kill a small crowd of people simply by running through it and creating a multi-man-kabob.

How to defeat them: Shoot them in the head or heart. Avoid getting stabbed. You can also feed them a bomb.

Bearigator

(Ursus Alligator Horribilis)

The bearigator is a massive creature with scales on their face, especially the snout, a tail used to trip its enemies, and huge claws that they use to rip open other creatures. The bearigator has 52 teeth, of which eight are large canines, and have the ability to take an elephant down with one bite. Bearigators usually remain in the vicinity of water, where they will eat other aquatic animals, sailors or scuba divers. Because they prefer larger prey, they gravitate toward sewers and ponds that give them access to humans.

Bearigators have amazingly fast reflexes and catch their prey by slapping their prey's legs with their tails and holding them down until they have broken their spine. Bearigators rarely chew their food. They bite to kill, then swallow.

The scales of a bearigator's tail sometimes fall off and are very sharp. These scales can be crafted into nearly unbreakable projectile weapons.

How to defeat them: Chain their tail and snout, then bash repeatedly with large rocks. Electrify the water they are in. Feed them bombs.

Bear Crab
(Ursus Liocarcinus vernalis)

The bear crab has been scientifically proven to give more nightmares than any other creature. It has claws, no paws, six pointy legs, and a hard exoskeleton. The bear crab's pincers are incredibly sharp and have the ability to cut a large man completely in half.

These crustaceans are ocean dwelling in nature and are dependent on salt water to survive. They live in beach caves near tourist beaches for sustenance and lay eggs deep in the sand. Bear crabs are all male and when it is time to reproduce, two male crabs battle and the one who loses becomes the female.

Bear crabs don't have any organs but brains, hearts, and gills that keep them alive. They are incredibly hard to kill and considered by some to be immortal.

How to defeat them: Bear crabs walk sideways, hindering the way they see. It is wise to attack them from the side, as they find it hard to turn around, but working in teams of two is best: one to distract the animal with a long stick and another to pierce their exoskeletons. The weakest point in the armor is between their legs and their exoskeleton. Bear crabs are much more agile in water and should only be attacked on land. You can also feed them bombs covered in fish heads.

Bear Bat
(Ursus acerodon jubatus)

The nocturnal bear bat is known for its massive black leathery wings. Bear bats cannot see very well in light and have sensitive ears that can follow the echoes of their roars. The creatures sleep in large caves or hollowed out buildings while hanging upside down. They sleep in groups of ten or more.

Bear Bats hunt during the night, mostly for humans. They hunt by catching their prey in their claws, then biting into their bodies with teeth that have a naturally occurring chloroform on them. The prey is carried back to their cave where the whole group will participate in killing and then eating it.

When mating season is upon them, the bear bats will go outside the caves and give a roar similar to what they use for echolocation. When a male and a female can mimic one another's roars perfectly, the two animals will mate and a cub will be born in due time. Bear bat cubs are born with very small wings and have to be taught how to fly. Bear bat cubs are very playful and enjoy capturing humans and dropping them from extremely high altitudes just to hear them scream.

How to defeat them: Invisible poisonous nets hung up high, day time cave bombings, Tesla coils, feed them a bomb.

Below: *A rare depiction of Axe Cop riding a tame bear bat while fighting zombies. Axe Cop bit the bear bat, which caused the creature to turn good. This is not recommended if you are not Axe Cop as it is very dangerous.*

Bearmadillo
(Ursus dasypus novemcinctus)

The bearmadillo is covered in armor formed by dermal bones. This armor covers their necks, backs, the top of their heads and their limbs while leaving the belly exposed. Their armor is also covered in sharp thorns.

The bearmadillo has very short legs with only three claws on each paw. Their long claws are like butcher knives and can cut a human to pieces easily. They move very fast and can also roll up into a ball and break through walls, roll through fires or over hot coals. It may also use the roll as an attack. If the victim is not crushed to death, the spikes on the bearmadillo's armor will pierce its body and the wound, being nearly impossible to close, will bleed out.

Bearmadillos have poor eyesight, but this makes them better hunters as they have to rely on their other senses, predominantly smell. They will smell you before you see them, so be ready to climb a tree. Bearmadillos are not good climbers.

If a bearmadillo captures you, it will close itself up around you. Once this happens you have no hope of escape. Once inside, the creature will suffocate you in the dark, then devour you. When it unrolls itself, it will scatter your bones.

How to defeat them: Trick them into rolling into hot lava, get them to wrap themselves around a bomb, hide underground and stab them in the belly when they walk by. Feed them bombs.

Tardigrizzly
(Ursus hypsibius dujardini)

The tardigrizzly is a megafauna water bear comparable in size to a blue whale. Its face is almost entirely dominated by its hose-shaped mouth which it uses to suck up prey like a vacuum cleaner, inhaling entire civilizations and defecating them into piles of glowing green mush. Tardigrizzlies are evolved from their microscopic cousin *tardigrada*, known for their ability to survive in deep space, atomic blasts and extreme temperatures. These bears can survive extreme pressures that you would find in only the deepest part of the oceans and radioactive emission that would kill all other species. They do not need oxygen to breathe.

While they can survive without food for centuries, it is in the tardigrizzly's nature to kill without ceasing. They can wipe out thousands of people or animals within minutes. They have six chubby legs that move slowly but can crush or climb over any surface.

The spines on their backs act as antennae that can also be used to communicate with other tardigrizzlies to formulate a global attack. The spines contain a viral poison that can be useful if weaponized, but can only be collected by wearing a suit made of oxidized iron and lambskin.

How to defeat them: Unknown

Grizzly Boar
(Ursus sus scrofa cristatus)

The grizzly boar is the size of an average grizzly bear with tusks coming from under its nose and sharp teeth on its bottom jaw. Its front legs end in paws with sharp claws that can rip enemies or prey limb from limb, while its hind legs have hooves for running and stomping. It lives in arid areas and burrows for nesting places, often fashioning caves out of piles of bones it has collected.

Males have larger canines than females and also omit an odor that causes vomiting of blood and eventual death. The odor secretes from a gland located in the humps on their backs, where urine and stomach bile mix to form a pungent, deadly acid.

How to defeat them: It is wise to attack a bear boar from behind, as their hind legs are underdeveloped and will give way easily. Avoid their tusks at all costs. Climbing trees is not a good way to avoid them because they can uproot them easily with their tusks. A spear down the throat or through the eye is best since they have such thick skin and bones. You can also feed them bombs.

Bear Duck
(Ursus Munoz superciliosa)

The bear duck is a semi-aquatic flightless bird-bear with dark, water-resistant fur, webbed claws, and a billed beak. The bears' front paws have sharp nails which make it easier to catch their prey whilst out of water and their back paws are large and have ankle spurs. The ankle spurs on females are venomous, unlike the male bear duck, and the venom consists of large amounts of ethanol and hydrochloric acid. The combination of gases coming from the animals make it hard for them to hunt for fish, as the fish will be poisoned or melted by the acid, which is why the males do the majority of hunting. The venom is created by the bear duck's immune system and comes in handy during their 24 month pregnancy. The venom is also used to kill humans.

These creatures have a diet consisting mainly of humans, but they also feed on large species of fish, water-dwelling monkeys and all breeds of dogs. Their bills are surprisingly strong and nearly impossible to pry open. The bear duck's quack is so loud your brain will kill itself.

How to defeat them: Use a duck call to lure them. Shoot them in the head or heart, but avoid hitting the bill because it is bulletproof. Can also be fed bombs.

13

Star Nosed Bear Mole
(Ursus condylura cristata)

The star nosed bear mole is one of the largest and most dangerous species of bear. While they have generally poor eyesight, they have large pink appendages on their snouts that work as eyes and ears as well as for smelling.

These creatures are found underground and can dig through almost anything. They get their sustenance from eating passers-by, bursting from the ground and snapping them up with their large teeth.

Despite their large size, star nosed bear moles are very sneaky and quiet. They can hear footsteps from as low as ten feet beneath the ground. They have tunnels leading everywhere that enable other bear species to travel unseen. But bear moles prefer to live in solitude, sometimes only with a mate. They only make sounds when attacking, creating a high pitched squeak roar that is nasal and ear piercing.

How to defeat them: The appendages on their noses are very sensitive and easy to cut off. A weed whacker is recommended. This will disorient the animal while you drive something sharp into its head. Can also be fed bombs.

Beaardvark
(Ursus orycteropus afer)

The Beaardvark is a species of bear that lives in burrows in the ground where they rear their young, avoiding rocky areas. This creature has a long, sticky tongue, pig-like snout, sharp claws, and powerful legs, which are shorter in the front than in the back. The powerful legs come in handy when digging burrows and the claws when breaking tree trunks in order to get to their prey. The beaardvark also has a keen sense of hearing, which is useful in their war on humans.

They are nocturnal creatures and, as a result, spend their days avoiding the heat in their burrows. During night time they hunt for sleeping people, biting into their throats and slurping out the insides with their long tongue.

Beaardvarks are also efficient in swimming and will likely be close to a water source.

How to defeat them: Set up a decoy of a sleeping person, fill it with bombs. You can also feed them bombs.

Tribearatops
(Ursus triceratops horridus)

It is a mystery how DNA of a triceratops was spliced with that of a bear to create this nearly unstoppable creature. Its back and belly are covered in fur while its legs and elongated tail are covered in hard, leathery skin. However, it's entire epidermal layer is nearly impenetrable. It has two sharp horns coming from its head and one smaller horn on its snout.

Many have tried to kill the tribearatops for the ivory protruding from their heads, but found the protrusions to be covered in a lethal oxytocin that causes death when touched. The tribearatops isn't a fast animal under normal circumstances. With one quick thrust of the head they can impale or decapitate an enemy. Attacking their young is a big mistake, as these creatures are very protective and maternal in nature.

These creatures have very firm and stout limbs that are heavy enough to kill by stomping. The tail, when swung, can send enemies to the ground who are then easily impaled on the creature's poisonous horns.

How to defeat them: There is a soft spot between the chest and belly that can be speared. Horns can be chained to a moving train. Also, feed it bombs.

Beargle
(Ursus Canis familiaris)

A beargle is a very large species of canine bear. It sports black, white and brown fur, with large floppy ears, a keen nose and alert eyes. Some believe these bears were bred to be guard dogs but no one has ever tamed one.

The beargle's ears are very sensitive. For protection, the animal hides poisonous spikes in its ears that will shoot into your body and pin you to the nearest tree or wall, where the creature will feast on your legs and feet.

The beargle attacks by biting your calves and thighs, causing you to fall down where it will proceed to chomp off your feet. The beargle does this to humans, cows and large species of birds, like ostriches and swans.

A female beargle can give birth to up to nineteen cubs. Never approach a mother beargle as this will be the last thing you ever do. The male beargle is the hunter for the family and is very loyal to his mate. If his mate is killed, he will seek out its killer at all costs. The male beargle will sometimes kill his own cubs if he feels they are taking time away from his mate.

How to defeat them: Kill the female, then set up a trap for the male. Can be speared through throat, head or heart. Can also feed them bombs.

Bearstrich

(Ursus struthio camelus)

The bearstrich is a tall and slender ursine bird with a feathered body, hairy legs and an elongated neck. The creatures were first discovered by Dr. Neal Powell, who was killed moments later. Despite its abnormal shape, the bearstrich is nonetheless a deadly species of bear, as it moves incredibly fast and will trip you when you run, shred you with its talons, and use its long neck to squeeze the life out of you.

These creatures live in packs of ten with the ratio divided equally between males and females. They can normally be found in sub-Saharan regions surrounded by grass and sand. They enjoy areas with wind as it alerts them to prey faster. The pack is an organized unit. Females make a warning sound before they attack, while males roar loudly. The sound coming from a female bearstrich can infiltrate your eardrums and cause them to burst. This act alone disorientates you and makes you, or any prey, easier to catch.

Bearstriches lay eggs in the sand and guard them while the males hunt. Beside human flesh, bearstriches also enjoy the taste of elephant feet, snake skins and the occasional wild boar.

How to defeat them: When you see a pack of bearstriches, running won't help. Instead, find a tree and get in it. For extra measures you can take off an article of clothing and wrap it around your head, specifically your ears, so that the female battle cry won't make your ears bleed. Try to lead them toward a sharp, taut wire that will decapitate them if they run through it. Can also feed them bombs.

Bear Trout
(Ursus salmo trutta)

The bear trout can only be found in freshwater rivers and lakes. Their bodies are covered in scales, usually white and orange, with large fins, and their faces are covered in fur with gills underneath their ears. Their scales are incredibly sharp and will easily cut a finger off if you aren't careful. They have large molars and canines and find it easy to eat other fish, snakes and even crocodiles or wading elk. When fully grown, a bear trout can chew through brick, rock, wood and steel, giving them the ability to take out underwater man-made structures.

Bear trout live in extended families that include up to twenty members, with a female as the school leader, the males as hunters, and other females doing their maternal duties. The males hunt for fish in groups of five. When hunting for a crocodile or any larger prey, the males all go together and carry it back to their homes in their mouths.

Bear trout are vicious creatures. They can devour all the flesh from your hand in mere seconds. A pair of large, thick leather gloves are advised when handling these creatures. If they don't eat you, their scales will chop off something important.

Furthermore, these creatures' young should be avoided, because they are born with incredibly sharp teeth that can chew through a human body in seconds.

How to defeat them: Fishing pole with a bomb on the hook.

Abearican Eagle
(Ursus Haliaeetus leucocephalus)

The Abearican Eagle is a creature that many Americans feel conflicted about. On one hand, it symbolizes their great nation, but it also eats your children. The Abearican Eagle is a species of bear with massive wings that can fly. Their bodies are covered in fur that gradually becomes feathers. Their feathers are resistant to very hot temperatures and fire, giving them the ability to swim through hot lava.

These creatures have fast reflexes and keen eyesight. They can see an ant when they're twenty three hundred feet in the air. They also have long talons that they use to catch their prey, which is almost exclusively human. They also catch deer, lions and zebras.

The Abearican Eagle lives in groups of three to four. They make caves their habitats, and are considered to be the king of all other bears. The females care for the cubs. They feed the cubs and look out for the other females, while the male does the hunting. When an Abearican Eagle female is expecting, the male pampers her by bringing her the bear equivalent of roses: piles of salmon. The Abearican Eagle is the gentleman of bears.

The Abearican Eagle is said to have had a role in American history. According to legend, President George Washington rode an Abearican Eagle into combat as part of the Continental Army in the American Revolutionary War. He started this dream of riding an Abearican Eagle into war when he began military service in the French and Indian War, though this technique was dismissed by his superiors. Washington was not happy about this. He dedicated his life to the study of the psyche of eagle bears and how to tame them. He took the secret to his grave.

When Washington was made commander-in-chief of the Continental army, he decided that horses weren't good steeds to fight upon since they couldn't attack enemies. He ordered some of his men to capture Abearican Eagles, which was not an easy task. The creatures were tamed by Washington himself and Washington formed a close bond with one specific bear who he named Leopold.

Much later, when the war was over and the Declaration of Independence signed, Washington made the Abearican Eagle the official animal of the United States of America, and commissioned a portrait of himself and the bear he'd ridden into combat with. However, after one of these creatures devoured endless numbers of the nation's youth, the official animal was changed to the bald eagle instead. None of this has been confirmed.

The Abearican Eagle is more than a vicious beast. It is also the symbol of hope for America that helped them escape from oppression. Factual or not, it is a symbol that anything can be attained if you try hard enough and do not give up.

How to defeat them: Spear through head, throat or heart. Feed them bombs.

Grizzle Glider

(Ursus petaurus breviceps)

The Grizzle glider frequents tall trees
and buildings. These creatures have large webs
of skin that stretch from their front paws to their
back paws. They use these webs to glide from one
surface to another in short distances. Grizzle gliders are
solitary creatures and are rarely found in groups. If two or
more are found together it is either mating season, which is
normally in summer and never lasts longer than a few weeks, or
it is a female and her cubs.

These creatures hunt by hiding in high places and swooping down onto their
prey. They love targeting picnics and campsites where people are relaxing near
trees. Sometimes the grizzle glider will hold its prey in its skin flaps, smothering
it in the elastic black skin and causing it to suffocate.

These animals won't enter a home under normal circumstances because they
do not like enclosed spaces. They also avoid water because their extra skin makes
it hard to swim. If a grizzle glider ends up submerged in water they will likely
drown. They also tend to be clumsy runners if they try to move too fast, which
is why they include lots of leaping and bounding if they want to cover a large
distance fast.

How to defeat them: Lure them into water. Hook their skin flaps and get them
tied up. Lure it into an enclosed space, then attack. Feed it bombs.

Bearnoceros
(Ursus Kesslerus Rhinocerotidae)

The bearnoceros can't see very far. It sees mostly blurs and shapes, but its sense of smell is amazing because it relies singularly on that sense to find and capture its prey. These animals live mainly on villagers, deer, zebras and large birds and are found in sub-Saharan areas. A wild bearnoceros should never be approached, as it will likely charge at you, and as long as you are on land it will chase you. You may climb a thick tree and hope for help, but these animals can uproot a tree with little effort. They hunt by charging at their prey, terrifying them with their icy breath and then impaling them with their horns.

While rhinoceros horns are useful for medicinal purposes, bearnoceros horns are to be avoided. These horns leak a type of acid that makes your heart stop within minutes or may cause your spine to fill with fluid which will make you unable to walk. You will also feel a burning sensation in your pelvic region for the remainder of your life.

The bearnoceros is a protective creature. The parents will level an entire forest to find their young. The male and female also share the hunting duties between them: one is the hunter while the other stays with the cub.

How to defeat them: Because of their thick armor it's best to feed them bombs.

Grizzly Hare

(Ursus lepus californicus)

The grizzly hare is a large animal with tall, pointy ears, oversized teeth, and big, padded, thickly clawed feet. These creatures hunt by causing a mini-earthquake as they hop violently. Meanwhile, their ears keep track of where their prey is going. They make soft sounds that can only be described as a roaring chatter. They also have sensitive noses that twitch uncontrollably when they sense the presence of potential prey.

Grizzly hares enjoy living in pairs, normally that of mother and cub. The father isn't in the picture for long; the female either chases him away or stomps him to death with her large feet. The male usually hops away and finds a new female, who will allow him to live with her for a short while until she has a cub and the same thing happens.

Grizzly hares catch their prey by lifting them off the ground with their teeth and smashing them against a nearby tree or wall. They may also pin the prey to the ground and stomp the life out of them with the big feet on their incredibly strong legs. The cub then enjoys a tender meal and slowly learns to chew tougher meat. Grizzly hares are found in more than one area, and can even be found in your backyard, seeing as they prefer the flesh of large dogs, cats and humans above all else. They travel by digging large tunnels that can pop up just about anywhere.

How to defeat them: Pour flammable liquid into their tunnels and light it, cut off their ears they will be unable to track you, feed them carrot shaped bombs.

Bearantula
(Ursus theraphosa blondi)

The bearantula is a species of bear that follows the arachnid line. It has eight large, hairy legs that each have the power to crush a human skull. Each leg is covered in bristly hairs that are shaken off when these creatures feel threatened, and when these hairs fall on you it feels as if you've fallen into a volcano. The heat will burn the flesh off your skin. Furthermore these animals have six eyes and can see in all directions. The bearantula has sharp upper teeth that it uses to chew its food, while it has two massive bear claws as lower teeth that hang from their mouths. These bear claws, or scientifically called their 'handibles', are important for these animals when hunting, as these are used to catch the prey and stuff it into their crunching teeth. The bearantula has a strong proclivity for the flavor of Pegasus meat. They build giant nets to capture the flying steeds then wrap them up in webbing like mummies. The bearantula inserts a proboscis into its prey that emits an acid that liquefies their innards, then it sucks the bloody stew back out of its prey, leaving behind a hollow, bony husk. These creatures live in forests and deserts. They also like to live near ranches, seeking out cattle to eat when winged horses are unavailable. In Mexico the bearantula has been called "the Chupacabra," the infamous goat sucker.

How to defeat them: Their webs are flammable and can be ignited while they are sleeping. If you can shoot out all six eyes they are easier to impale. There is a soft spot just between the thorax and abdomen on their under side. Also, you can feed them bombs.

Bear Frog
(Ursus lithobates catesbeianus)

Bear frogs are a massive species of amphibious bear. Born in the water, they metamorphose from a legless tadcub. They are born from clusters of slimy, hairy eggs and usually do not exceed more than three per hatching period, seeing as the other eggs are all eaten by the hungry firstborns. As a tadcub, the bear frog is underdeveloped and only has a set of gills to breathe through, making water vitally important. At seven weeks the tadcub's lungs are fully developed and it can emerge from the water. At nine weeks, it is now a bear frog with fully developed teeth and claws and ready to hunt for itself. Prey includes fishermen, pythons, alligators, parachutists, and wildlife that drink from the water. The bear frog female does the hunting: she excretes a pungent scent that causes the prey to become unconscious. This smell doesn't affect other bear frogs or tadcubs. At eleven weeks, the bear frog leaves its home in search of a family of its own.

Bear frogs are found in swamps, rivers and lakes. When desperate, they will wander into a civilized area and catch prey there, usually humans or domesticated pets. They will blend in with greenery and sit completely still, then catch unsuspecting passersby with their sticky, elastic tongue.

While female bear frogs give off a smell that knocks you unconscious, the male bear frog prefers to literally knock your head completely off. It is larger than the female and its claws, when swiped at the head, can cause decapitation.

How to defeat them: A bear frog can be blinded with very bright light, causing it to freeze. There skin is easy to penetrate as long as you don't hit bone. Try to pop their chin sack to obstruct their breathing. A bomb made up to look like a large fly also can work.

Bearwhal
(Ursus monodon monoceros)

The bearwhal is a salt water mammal, originating around Canadian coasts and the seas surrounding Greenland. They are known as the unicorn of the bear species due to the large horns they have on their foreheads – it is this horn that the bearwhals use in both hunting and mating rituals. Males engage in duels each year to attract mates. These sword fights usually end up with one of the creatures losing their horns, or half of it, and being cast out of the bearwhal community for a whole year. The females then choose whether they are happy with the winning bearwhals. If they are, everything goes great. If they're not, it will look like the ten plagues hit Canada. Bearwhal females are very fussy when it comes to their mates.

Furthermore, bearwhals hunt in groups, spearing their prey by impaling them with their horns. Once prey has been speared, another bearwhal will help it get the prey off once they return to their homes, which are found in underwater caves filled with seaweed and rocks. Common prey include the Arctic cod and the Greenland halibut, with scuba divers and mermaids often being victims as well.

Young bearwhals are born without their horns. These grow later. The young are usually coddled by their mothers and hidden in the caves until their horns have grown out, which is when they will be ready for their own mating rituals. It is rumored that the bearwhal's horn is actually a long tusk. Bull crap.

How to defeat them: A speeding bearwhal can get stuck in a board like a dart if the wood is thick enough and it hits at full speed. Never try to cut the horn off of a live bearwhal; it's impossible. When possible, feed them bombs.

Bearboon
(Ursus papio anubis)

The Bearboon is known for its screech and the disastrous effects it has on humans and animals alike. The hybrid has a large body covered in thick yellow and gray fur, with a face reminiscent of a bear, but with a long, snarling snout. The bearboon is a symbol of power to the natives living on the continent of Africa. It is usually found in grassy lands with tall grass that makes it easier to stalk their prey. Bearboons focus mainly on attacking people riding in safari jeeps wearing little round hats.

The male prefers to do the hunting. Their screech is so powerful that, when directed at an unsuspecting animal, their flesh will be blown off, leaving behind only blood and bones. The bearboons aren't too fussy about what they eat as long as they get food. The females have a terrifying screech as well, but it won't cause death, it will simply cause their male mates to become furious and defensive.

The most shocking aspect of the Bearboon is its giant reddish-purple booty. It looks like a 50 pound wad of chewing gum with hair in it and, though it cannot harm you, it is no comfort that if the Bearboon devours you, it's horrible red, lump anus will be your only means of escape.

How to defeat them: Stay far away, using guns only, or feed them bombs.

Beartoise
(Ursus aldabrachelys gigantea)

Not to be confused with the beartle, the beartoise is a hybrid that has a rock hard shell covering its back and belly. Unlike their cousin, the tortoise, these creatures are extremely agile: they tuck themselves into their shells and roll down mountains, knocking over trees and crushing anything in their path. These creatures have the ability to control how they move and can survive in both extreme cold and heat. They build nests made from dark granite, demolished buildings and the bones of their prey.

The beartoise also lives in solitude, mating only once every fifteen years before moving back into their caves of death. These creatures tend to feast on foxes, mountain lions, and humans. One flaw these creatures have is that they cannot survive without their shells, because it forms part of their exoskeleton, meaning their organs are left exposed if the shell would be removed. Attempting to remove the shell while the beast is still alive is not advised. The other flaw the beartoise possesses is the fact that its teeth aren't nearly as sharp as any of its predecessors, but they possess a hard beak that can bite through bone or tree trunks with ease.

How to defeat them: Try to use fire to make them hide in their shell, then put a bomb inside. Their neck and eyes are about the only place a spear can do damage, but they can chomp a spear to splinters so be careful. It's best if you can feed it a bomb.

Bear Moth
(Ursus attacus atlas)

The bear moth prefers to come out at night. It is nocturnal and one of the few species of bear that are drawn to light. So, to avoid these bears, it would be wise to turn off the lights at night.

Bear moths are born as bear caterpillars from massive larvae found in underground tunnels. In the caterpillar state they have eight legs, teeth, and a constant craving for crocodile flesh. They're usually found in sewers or underground railway stations. After two months, the caterpillar weaves itself into a cocoon made from crocodile skin, or even cow skin if crocodiles aren't available.

Another month passes and these creatures emerge as bear moths. At this stage they sport white, spindly wings and when they fly, they appear to be broken. A broken bear moth wing is a rare find and are said to cure many diseases, so if you find one, grind it up with rocks and keep it in a small container. It may come in handy.

Bear moths prefer to eat softer meat than that of the crocodile, so they fly out from the sewers and tunnels in order to find it. Usually the prey ends up being humans, cows, donkeys, horses and deer. Bear moths can't see that well and will leave smaller creatures like dogs and cats alone.

How to defeat them: Bear moths are one of the easiest bear hybrids to defeat. By drawing them into a light you can pick them off one by one. They are incredibly stupid and easy to fool. Though you can also feed them bombs.

Bearakeet
(Ursus melopsittacus undulatus)

The bearakeet has the ability to turn its head all the way around, 360 degrees. It has yellow, beady eyes that can see in the dark. The bearakeet has a large, feathered body with extremely sharp talons, along with a wingspan of 9 feet and stands over 8 feet tall. The head consists of a pair of yellow eyes, as mentioned, and small ears. These ears make the bearakeet look almost friendly, but pay it no mind as this is how the animal catches their prey. The bearakeet is an animal that relies on the fact that it is adorable to lure their prey.

The bearakeet also uses mimicry to fool its prey. It can imitate any sound it hears, so it may imitate a cat's meow, or a scared child to lure in human prey. When a flock has finished devouring a person they will all mimic the cries of the dying prey in celebration.

Bearakeets live in large trees, typically in families of three. Cubs are live birthed and the female bearakeets are, interestingly enough, much more attractive than the male with brighter colors and a call that sounds like the most beautiful melody. Males flock to them and the result is a bear equivalent of polygamy, with a female having more than one mate. Female bearakeets mostly snack on creatures in trees, like snakes and monkeys, but males do the hunting, bringing back teams of loggers and rangers to feast on.

How to defeat them: The bearakeet will spend hours staring at itself in a mirror. Use that as a distraction then shoot them in the head. Feeding them bombs, however, is a horrible idea.

About the Author

Dickinson Killdeer

Dickinson Killdeer does not remember much of his life. All he remembers is waking up in the forest one day. He lives by the only two books he could find among his belongings, a Boy Scout manual and a pocket Bible. While lost in the forest, Killdeer observed the ways of animals. Over time, he noticed the strange behaviors and mutations of the bears and realized that they were headed toward civilization to wipe out mankind. Killdeer followed the bears for two reasons: to find his way back to humanity, and to save it.

SUBSCRIBE TO ETHAN NICOLLE ON

Name your price and pledge monthly to keep Ethan Nicolle making stuff like this! In return you get...

• **FREE digital version** of everything I make, or have made that exists in digital format.
• **Early releases** of everything I make
• **All printed items at my cost** you pay what I pay to print books
• **Signed and sketched in**: every book I sell patrons will get a free sketch.
• **Tips and tutorials** on art and writing
• **Exclusive first looks** at projects I can't post publicly
• **Sketches** and rare art
• **Live, interactive video** streams in group and one on one
• **Commissions,** sketches, custom avatars...
• **More!** You could even be a character in every project I ever make.

VISIT WWW.PATREON.COM/ETHANNICOLLE FOR MORE INFO

OTHER BOOKS BY ETHAN NICOLLE

BEARMAGEDDON VOL. 1

BEARS HAVE DECLARED WAR ON ALL HUMANS. Joel and his slacker friends get caught in the midst of an all-out war on mankind by bears. Their only hope is a grizzled mountain man with an axe named Dickinson Killdeer.

CHUMBLE SPUZZ

Eisner nominated for Best Humor Publication in 2009, *Chumble Spuzz* is a collection of insane stories about two strange friends who do things like try to kill Satan and help a chicken get free cookies. Published by **SLG Publishing**.

AXE COP

Created by Ethan Nicolle and his 5 year old brother, *Axe Cop* went on to become an animated TV show on **FOX**. Published by **Dark Horse Comics**, *Axe Cop* comes in six volumes, collecting the web comic and the three print-exclusive miniseries.

Made in the
USA
Lexington, KY